Merry Merry
Huckleberry

OTHER YEARLING BOOKS YOU WILL ENJOY:

HELLO HUCKLEBERRY HEIGHTS, Judy Delton
SUMMER SHOWDOWN, Judy Delton
THE ARTIFICIAL GRANDMA, Judy Delton
HUCKLEBERRY HASH, Judy Delton
SCARY SCARY HUCKLEBERRY, Judy Delton
BACK YARD ANGEL, Judy Delton
ANGEL IN CHARGE, Judy Delton
ANGEL'S MOTHER'S BOYFRIEND, Judy Delton
ANGEL'S MOTHER'S WEDDING, Judy Delton

YEARLING BOOKS/YOUNG YEARLINGS/YEARLING
CLASSICS are designed especially to entertain and enlighten
young people. Patricia Reilly Giff, consultant to this series,
received the bachelor's degree from Marymount College. She
holds the master's degree in history from St. John's University,
and a Professional Diploma in Reading from Hofstra University.
She was a teacher and reading consultant for many years, and
is the author of numerous books for young readers.

For a complete listing of all Yearling titles, write to
Dell Readers Service, P.O. Box 1045,
South Holland, IL 60473.

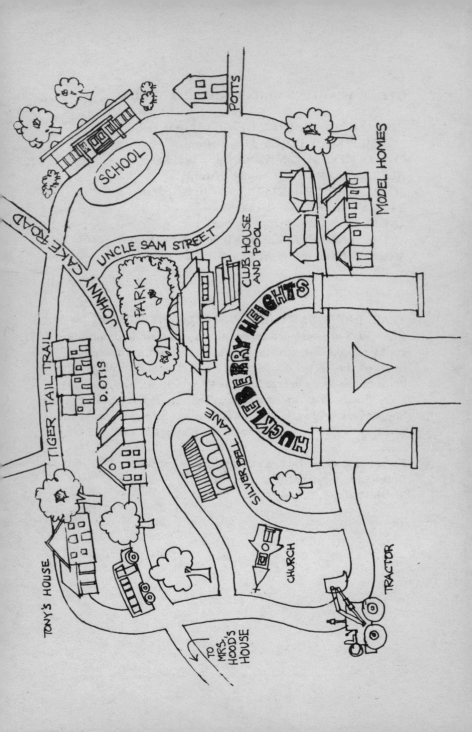

Merry Merry Huckleberry

Judy Delton

Illustrated by Alan Tiegreen

A YEARLING BOOK

FOR LORNA AND JOHN BALIAN:
WITH WARM MEMORIES OF OUR
THANKSGIVING IN SEPTEMBER

Published by
Dell Publishing
a division of
Bantam Doubleday Dell Publishing Group, Inc.
666 Fifth Avenue
New York, New York 10103

ISBN: 0-440-40365-0

Printed in the United States of America

November 1990

10 9 8 7 6 5 4 3 2 1

CWO

1

"There's no news but snow news," said the weather reporter on my radio, laughing. "And snow news is not good news," he continued.

It's good news if my school is closed, I wanted to tell him. Snow news could be good news.

I flipped the dial around to find a station that had a guy who wasn't telling jokes. I wanted to hear words like *Tony Doyle's school in Huckleberry Heights will be closed today*. A serious guy. A day off was not a joking matter.

One station didn't mention the snow at all. "So come in and get your car needs for half price." I didn't have car needs, I had free-day needs.

The next station was playing hymns, and WCCO said there was a smokers' seminar at a St. Paul auditorium at three o'clock.

I looked out of my bedroom window, and let me tell you, none of those smokers were going to get there. Unless they went on a dogsled. Or maybe a snowmobile. Or in Santa's sleigh.

I went into my sister Marcy's room in my pajamas. "Wait till you look outside," I said. "The drifts are up to the windowsills."

Marcy groaned in her sleep. "I have to get to my ballet lesson," she said.

"It'll be canceled," I said cheerfully, walking down the hall to my little brother Gus's room.

"No school today," I announced.

Gus raced to the window. "Oh, boy," he said. "I can make a fort out there." But he crawled back into bed, and I decided to do the same thing. It was still dark outside.

There's nothing nicer than scrunching down under a quilt all snuggly and

2

warm when it's snowing out and you know you should be in school. Kind of like cheating legally.

"Anthony," said a voice at my door. The voice had a frown. "I am going to try to get to work. You listen to the radio and find out if the schools are closed. If they don't announce it, you better get up and get an early start."

"Okay. Good-bye, Mom."

I turned over and pulled the quilt over my ears. I turned the dial on my radio again.

"The smokers' seminar at the St. Paul Auditorium will be canceled until next week," the same voice said.

I turned my radio off. Didn't I tell you those smokers couldn't get through all that snow? I didn't need to listen to the radio for school closings. No little kids could trudge through a blizzard like this.

This is the first winter we've lived out here in Huckleberry Heights. We used to live in St. Paul in an apartment, but last spring my mom decided we needed a yard and a barbecue and more room and a tree, so she bought this condo (short for condominium). A condo is just like a real house except that it is four houses hitched together under one roof. We have our own yard and garden and driveway and garage, and when you're inside you can't tell the difference between a condo and a house.

Our school is just a few blocks away, but my mom has to drive in to St. Paul to work; she has her own company called Trixie's Taps. She makes faucets. She loves faucets. Her whole life is faucets. Chrome and copper and even gold ones.

The phone rang and I answered it. "Do you think there's school today?" asked my friend Edgar Allan Potts.

"Naw," I said. "We're in the middle of a blizzard. They couldn't expect those little first-graders to get to school."

Edgar and I are ten. We are in fifth grade. Marcy is twelve and Gus is eight.

"They didn't announce it on the radio," said Edgar.

"What do they know?" I said.

"My mom said to call you," Edgar went on. "She said she never knows what's going to happen with the weather in Minnesota."

That's what everyone says in Minnesota. You can't tell from one minute to the next what will happen.

"Trust me," I said. "I'm going back to bed."

I hung up and looked in at Marcy, and at Gus. They were both snoring.

I took a look out the window. There didn't seem to be any more snow coming down, but there was enough on the ground already to last a year. The snowplow was stuck in a drift down the street in front of my girlfriend Lily Camp's house.

I watched TV awhile and then read some old comic books. I went to the kitchen and ate some cereal, and then I crawled into bed again.

I'll just take a little nap, I thought, and then I'll get up and make a fort with Gus. If we can even open the back door.

As I dozed off I dreamed about the

summer in Huckleberry Heights. I was riding my bike and going to the pool and running my sheepdog, Smiley. I could feel the wind in my hair and see Smiley's ears flying in the breeze. I thought I heard Edgar calling me to swim.

All of a sudden I woke up. How long had I been asleep? Was the whole day gone? Did Gus build a fort without me?

I leapt to my feet and ran into his room. His bed was made and he was gone.

I ran into Marcy's room. She was gone too. So were her ski jacket and book bag and ballet shoes.

"Where is everybody?" I called. "Marcy? Gus?"

My voice seemed to echo in the empty house. I whipped on my jeans and ran to the front door. When I opened the door, the thing I noticed first was the bright bright sunlight. There was snow on the ground, but it was melting fast. The streets were clear and condo workers must have shoveled the sidewalks and driveways.

"Where is my blizzard?" I yelled out

the door. "What happened to the snow-storm?"

The clock said ten o'clock. I had this awful feeling in the bottom of my stomach. I was the only one in Huckleberry Heights who wasn't in school today.

How was I supposed to know the blizzard would disappear while I took a nap? And why didn't someone tell me? What kind of family did I have?

I had two choices. I could stay home and say I had been sick. But I'd need a note from my mom, and how would I get her to lie? Especially when she'd told me to listen to the radio to be sure school was closed.

My other choice, of course, was to go to school and face the music. I might as well get it over with. I got my jacket and ran down the street. All these mothers were out walking their babies in strollers and buggies, and they looked at me as if I were from a foreign land. It was a foreign land. I was a stranger in a land of parents and babies and daytime soaps. A place where people hung clothes

on the line and had coffee in each other's kitchens and where school kids didn't belong.

I was all out of breath when I got to my room. Mr. Cummings, our principal, was standing in the hall, but I snuck around him.

"Why, Anthony," said Miss Roscoe as I slid in the door. All the kids looked at me. "We thought you must be ill today."

"I stayed home because of the blizzard," I said. The class tittered. They didn't have to rub it in. I could see the sun. "How did I know it would end so fast?" I said.

"You can't trust the weather in Minnesota, Anthony," said my teacher. "It changes very quickly from one minute to the next."

"Yes, Miss Roscoe," I said, feeling like a fool who couldn't tell when it was snowing out.

"I think we can all learn something from this," Miss Roscoe went on. "We all must listen to WCCO to get the school closings. Unless you hear the name of our school on the air, school will be in session."

"It isn't even snowing," said Lily when I sat down.

"You gave me a bum steer," said Edgar. "I was all ready to stay home when my mom said, 'Tony must be wrong.' "

At lunchtime I couldn't wait to get my hands on Marcy and Gus.

"We called you when we left," said Marcy, doing some ballet step in the cafeteria line. "And you didn't budge."

"Tony's scared of snowflakes," sang Punkin Head Maloney when he saw me. He is in between Gus and me in school because he flunked kindergarten. He's kind of round, that's why he gets called Punkin Head.

At three o'clock we had a snowball fight and I won, and that night we had more snow that really was a blizzard. My mom came in all white like a snowman and said, "Why do we live in Minnesota? You can't tell from one minute to the next what the weather is going to do!"

2

By morning there was no doubt about a free day. Every single radio station was blaring, "All schools in the area are closed due to last night's blizzard." My mother woke us up early.

"It's a perfect day for taking a picture for our Christmas card," she said. "Our friends out of town will see what a real Minnesota winter is like!"

"They'll think we live in Antarctica," groaned Marcy. "I don't want my friends to think we live in an igloo."

My mom was getting her camera off the closet shelf. She opened it and put the film in. I could hear the click click click of the little holes going onto the sprockets.

"I have thirty-six exposures on this film," she said. "We have to take a lot of them so we can pick the best."

"You mean in case Gus makes a crazy face," I said.

"Or Tony has his eyes closed," muttered Marcy.

"Thirty-six pictures will allow a margin for error," said my mother. She set the camera on the hall table and snapped her fingers. "Breakfast," she said. "I forgot to make your breakfast."

We all dragged out of bed and ate my mom's oatmeal and put on the most wintry-looking clothes we had.

"The door won't open!" shouted Gus.

"It's ten below zero!" said Marcy.

"What a perfect day to capture Minnesota on film!" said my mother.

I had to admit Mom was right. Once we got the door open, it was like being on a desert. A desert of snow. We all sank in to our hips when we tried to walk. Smiley and Gus couldn't walk at all! I cleared a little path for them, and then Gus dived into a snowbank as if it

was a swimming pool, and in five minutes he and Smiley looked like snow monsters.

The wind had blown the snow into giant drifts of hills and valleys, and for as far as I could see no one had walked in it. It was like uncharted territory, snow exactly where nature dumped it. And all of it, the whole Huckleberry Heights of it, sparkled like Marcy's imitation diamond necklace.

"You can't see the street!" yelled Gus. "Where is Tiger Tail Trail?"

"It never snowed this much before," I said. "This must be the worst blizzard of the century."

My mom shook her head. "We just didn't notice before," she said. "Because we lived in the city. There are so many buildings and so many people, the snow never got a chance to stay where it fell."

All of a sudden I saw something moving. It looked like a red hat. The hat was making a path toward our house.

"Lenny!" shouted Gus. "That's Lenny's hat!"

Gus was right. Lenny Fox dragged himself toward us and collapsed at our feet. He was all out of breath. He lived a few blocks away on Johnny Cake Road.

"I was lost in the wilderness," he panted. "I couldn't tell where you lived. The mailboxes are all covered up."

"Let's take the pictures," said Marcy. "I'm freezing out here."

"Can Lenny be in the pictures?" asked Gus.

"Of course," said my mother, looking through her little viewfinder at us. "I think you should all get behind that big drift in the driveway."

"All the drifts are big," I said. It was a long way to the driveway.

By the time my mom had us the way she wanted us, Punkin Head had come down the hill on his toboggan, and Lily Camp had plowed up to our house too.

There was a whole line of kids in the picture by the time my mom snapped it. Smiley was right in front. He was like a snowball, gathering more and more snow as he rolled in it. By the time we snapped him, he'd become a regular snow elephant.

"We need some props," said my mother. "Something to give the picture color. And a Christmas look."

My mom made us all trudge back into the house and up to the attic to find the props. She made Gus put on a little Santa Claus suit. Then she carried a small artificial Christmas tree down to set in the drift. "Our trees out here are just too short. They are all covered up with snow."

Marcy wrote *Merry Christmas* in the drift in front of us. It was a lot of work. The snow was so deep.

"It looks just right," said my mother at last. "Line up."

Thirty-six is a lot of pictures. My mom kept moving us around, which was silly because all there was was snow anyway. By number thirty-six, none of us could smile anymore or pretend we were having fun in a Minnesota winter. My toes were frozen solid.

We all went in, and Mom made us

hot cocoa and lit a fire in the fireplace.

"Right now," said Punkin Head, looking at his Mickey Mouse watch, "we would be having spelling. Yuck."

It was hard to believe it was a school day. A little nature in Minnesota could really mess up the schedule.

By noon the snowplows were out, and when they finally went by, the snow was piled up on the boulevards higher than the cars, higher even than the school buses. In place of the snow in the street was solid ice. The radio warned people not to drive. We were just into a game of Scrabble when who should come sailing down the street on ice skates but Edgar.

"Come on!" he called. "It's a giant skating rink!"

I ran down to the basement and found our box of skates. Lily wore an old pair of Marcy's that she'd outgrown. Edgar skated to Lenny's house to get his skates. Pretty soon all of Huckleberry Heights was out skating up and down driveways, down the middle of the streets,

past the clubhouse and pool, and even right up to the door of our school! Lily's dad took pictures of us so we could remember this moment in case it never came again.

"This is going to be some winter," he said. "It isn't even Christmas yet!"

Marcy's friend Daisy came over from next door and all of us built a fort and had a snowball fight. We made angels in the snow and rolled giant snowballs for snowmen and snow women.

"Hey," yelled Edgar to Punkin Head. "Yours looks just like you!"

He was right. Punkin Head's snowman was big and round and had a snow candy bar in its hand.

Lily made two snowpeople holding hands. "It's us," she said. "Isn't it romantic?" My face got all red. It always does when she says mushy stuff like that. No one could tell this time because of the cold.

At three o'clock the streets were sanded and cars were going by.

"I'm going to the mall," called my

mother. "With Mrs. Otis. I want to get our pictures developed at the one-hour shop."

We waved good-bye and Daisy asked us all to come over to her house to make fudge for a candy sale her class was having. Marcy was buying oatmeal bars.

"It's supposed to be homemade," said Daisy. "It won't take long with all of us working at it."

Daisy got all the ingredients out of the cupboard. "Yum," said Punkin Head. "Do we get some if we help?"

"One piece," said Daisy. She poured cocoa and sugar in a pan. She got walnuts out. Lily got out a bag of flour.

"There's no flour in fudge!" I yelled. What kind of a wife would Lily be? I'd starve to death.

"It makes fudge get thick," said Lily.

"Pooh," said Lenny.

We took turns stirring the fudge. Everyone got a turn and then they got another one.

"How long does this stuff take?" said Edgar.

"Till it forms a ball in cold water," said Marcy.

Daisy kept dropping some in water and it kept disappearing. We kept stirring the pan on the stove. It looked like chocolate milk.

"I told you it needed flour," said Lily.

"If you put in flour, it will turn into cake," said Marcy.

"This is a candy sale," said Daisy.

Smiley began to sniff the air. He has a good nose.

"What's burning?" I said.

Daisy grabbed a hot pad and took the pan off the stove.

"It's not done and it's burning," she said.

I looked in the pan. It wasn't like chocolate milk anymore. It was like chocolate jam. Daisy poured the nuts in.

"It just needs to cool," said Lenny helpfully. Lenny was usually right. He knows a lot.

Daisy poured the fudge into a cake pan and set it out in the snow in the backyard. We all licked the pot. It tasted good even if it was runny. We washed the dishes and put stuff away, and went out to see if Lenny was right. He wasn't. The fudge was still thin. Way too thin to cut.

"I have an idea," I said. "We can make sandwiches out of it."

"Fudge sandwiches?" cried Daisy.

Everyone but Punkin Head pooh-poohed the idea, but they could see the stuff was too thick to drink and too thin to eat with your fingers.

Daisy got a loaf of bread out of the bread box. We spread slices with fudge and slapped other slices on top of each.

"Delicious!" said Punkin Head.

"It makes it go farther," said Edgar.

"The bread does hold the fudge together," said Lenny.

"I suppose I could cut the crusts off to make it look fancy," said Daisy. "Maybe they will think it's a new recipe."

"Have you got a cookie cutter?" asked Marcy.

Daisy got out little cutters in the shape

of hearts and butterflies and diamonds. We all cut shapes out of the sandwiches. Little butterfly and heart fudge sandwiches.

"They don't look bad," Daisy admitted.

"And with the bread, these could be either for a candy sale, or for a bake sale," said Lenny, with his mind for business.

Daisy had just covered the tray of fudge sandwiches with foil when our mothers walked in, full of snow. My mother didn't look happy. It didn't seem like the time to bring up the fudge fiasco.

"Let's see the pictures," I said.

"Are we all smiling?" asked Gus.

"None of you is smiling," said my mother. "There are no Christmas pictures. I left the lens cap on the camera and we have to do it all over again."

All of a sudden I was tired of winter. And it was just beginning.

3

The next morning the radio man said, "It's a bright winter morning and all the roads are open again after the big blizzard. Watch for icy spots on the pavement, motorists. And good news for the youngsters too—ha ha ha—the schools are open! So roll out of bed, you kids . . ."

I hated to be called a "youngster." What if somebody called that guy an oldster? I wonder how he'd like it.

When we were all dressed for school in our jackets and scarves and boots, my mom lined us up in front of the house for another picture. This time she said, "No props, no background, no thirty-six poses."

"And no lens cap," said Marcy.

My mom snapped one picture and we all were smiling, all three of us, and I was careful to check that the lens cap was off.

"That will do it," said my mom, putting her camera away. I could see she had lost interest in picture taking.

When we got to school, there was a big Santa Claus on our classroom door. Miss Roscoe had a big smile on her face.

"Good morning, boys and girls!" she said. "Sit down quickly, I have all kinds of news."

Edgar looked excited about the word *news*. I was suspicious. News came in good and bad, and even if it sounded good, it often ended up bad, I found.

Miss Roscoe leaned against her desk in the front of the room. She looked pink and happy, the way grown-up people did when they had a new boyfriend or girlfriend.

"The holidays," whispered Miss Roscoe as if they were a deep dark secret, "are almost upon us."

Was that all? Thanksgiving was over, and everyone in the room knew that Christmas and New Year's were coming next. That may be good news since a vacation came with them, but it sure was no surprise.

"I have several pieces of holiday news today," Miss Roscoe went on.

A buzz went around the room. Lily drew pictures of fir trees in her notebook. With presents under them.

"First of all, I thought it would be fun to draw names out of a hat and exchange gifts with a classmate. Then on the last day of school before vacation, we will have a little party and open packages. It will be very festive." She looked at us for response.

"I don't have any money," shouted Lucas.

"That's the good part," said Miss Roscoe. "You don't need money for this present. You will bring something that you make yourself! It will be an exercise in creativity, as well as a gift to bring joy to a friend."

The class moaned. Miss Roscoe's face fell. It was not the reaction she was looking for, I could see that.

"I'm not creative," said Lily firmly. "My mom said so."

"We are all creative," said Miss Roscoe, whose face was turning from pink to red. "Creativity must be nurtured, like a fine hothouse flower. We must tend our garden in order to bloom."

I don't know about Miss Roscoe, but I didn't want to bloom. And I didn't want a pot holder some kid made for a Christmas present.

"Can we buy the present if we save our money up?" I asked.

Miss Roscoe shook her head violently. "Absolutely not," she said. "Something homemade, from the heart, is far more valuable than anything mere money can buy."

She gave *mere money* a nasty twist with her voice that made me shiver. I liked money fine. She made it sound negative. It would serve her right if she got a deskful of pot holders for Christmas and nothing else.

"We will all make something lovely for the person whose name we draw, and that's that," said our teacher heatedly.

We groaned again.

"I think some of us have attitude problems in this room," said Miss Roscoe. She stared at Lily and me. And some other loud groaners.

We sat politely and waited for the second piece of bad news.

"The next news is about our Christmas play," said Miss Roscoe, trying to make a new start.

I couldn't believe it, but the class groaned again. It was like a habit now. We would have groaned at anything she said because it riled her so much. Teachers bring out the worst in you.

"Stop that!" she shouted. "The holidays are a happy time for fun and mirth and we are going to have a good time even if . . ."

Here her voice trailed off into some low-key threat.

A teacher's job is not a happy one. I'll

have to remember to be something like a janitor or a nuclear physicist—not a teacher. It's really thankless.

"I thought we'd present a short version of Dickens's *A Christmas Carol.*" She held up her hand as if to ward off blows from the audience. But no one ever heard of *A Christmas Carol,* so they just stared. "I know it's a bit much for one small class to do," she went on, "but I like a challenge, don't you, boys and girls?"

"Can I be Carol?" said someone in the back of the room.

Now it was Miss Roscoe who groaned. She held up a book. On the cover was a picture of this guy dragging some chains. It looked as if it was from a TV show my mom won't let me watch. I wondered if my mom knew what Miss Roscoe was teaching us.

"This author," she said, "is very very famous. This is the story of Bob Cratchit and Tiny Tim and Scrooge and Marley."

She waited for the class to recognize these names.

"I saw Tiny Tim on TV," shouted Edgar. "He sings."

"That is a different Tiny Tim," said our teacher. She looked as if she was going to cry now, even if it was close to the fun-filled holidays.

"How many Tiny Tims could there be?" whispered Edgar. "It's not a popular name."

"I want all of you to get this book from a library or store and read it—or have your parents read it to you—as soon as possible," said Miss Roscoe. "Before I give out the parts."

The class sighed. Extra homework did not seem in keeping with the holiday spirit.

"The next piece of news is that there will be a holiday pet show given by the lower grades, our grade and the second, third, and fourth. We meet in the auditorium after lunch so Mr. Cummings can tell you about it."

I could see Miss Roscoe was crestfallen now. She was a defeated woman, rattling off announcements the way they did at a pet show, with no enthusiasm. She was not even trying to sound excited.

"We are lucky to be in a school where there is so much holiday fun," she said. "A party with presents, a Christmas play, and a pet show all in the same month."

We all clapped, but it was mercy clapping. We had to get Miss Roscoe out of the doldrums. If she was moody, she'd be mean. If she was mean, she'd give us more homework. If we had more homework, it could ruin Christmas. She might even give us homework over vacation!

At lunch I ran into Punkin Head in the cafeteria. He had his plate loaded with lots of Jell-O because it had marshmallows in it. His teacher had talked about the pet show too.

"I don't have a pet," said Punkin Head. "Not a single pet."

"You can share Smiley," I said. "If we have to bring a pet, you can have half of him. He's big enough for two."

Punkin Head shook his head. "I want my own," he said. "I want something better than a dog or a cat."

"There is nothing better than a dog," I said in Smiley's defense. I was glad he wasn't here to hear Punkin Head's words. "I'm going to dress him up, or tie a red bow on his neck and ears."

Punkin Head looked miserable. I knew how he felt. It would be a lousy life without a pet.

As for me, I couldn't wait to hear what Mr. Cummings had to say. I would wash and brush and comb Smiley and practice up his fetching and situps. If there was a winner in this holiday pet show, my dog was going to be it.

4

"He's my dog too," said Gus when he heard me volunteering half a dog to Punkin Head. "If we have to bring a pet, half of him is mine."

I suppose he was right. I knew my mom wouldn't like the idea of buying another dog just so we'd each have our own entry.

"Okay," I said. "But you have to help get him ready. You have to wash your half."

At two o'clock all the lower grades filed into the auditorium. Miss Roscoe was right, you could tell the holidays were coming. We missed a whole geography lesson because of going to the auditorium to listen to Mr. Cummings talk about the holiday pet show. And we'd miss more by the time we drew names out of a hat for holiday gifts and practiced for the holiday play.

"The holidays," boomed Mr. Cummings's voice over the loudspeaker, "are only weeks away. We here at Huckleberry Heights Elementary School want to make the holidays as exciting as possible."

"They must take happy-holiday lessons," whispered Lenny in my ear. "My teacher said the same thing."

"One of our first holiday events here at H.H. Elementary," said our principal, "will be the primary grades pet show. We will have it here in our auditorium, which will be decorated by the sixth-graders for the occasion. If you have a pet, bring it! If it can do a trick, we'll watch it. If it can't do a trick, teach it one now!"

Hands were waving in the air.

"Can we bring more than one pet?" asked Lenny Fox.

"Bring one, bring all!" said Mr. Cummings.

"I have a trained goldfish," said one first-grader. "But he can't breathe out of water."

"Bring his bowl," boomed Mr. Cummings.

"I have a gerbil," said a girl from Gus's room. "But he can't do anything."

"Bring it anyway," said Mr. Cummings. "Just because your pet can't do a trick doesn't mean it isn't welcome."

The girl looked happy. I'll bet a lot of pets can't do tricks. My dog is one of the talented ones.

Mr. Cummings talked on about the date and the time and how the animals should act. (They couldn't bite people or chew up the furniture.) Then he said, "Now I'd like to get an idea of how many pets will be in this show, so I'll ask you to tell me now the pet you plan to bring."

He pointed to Edgar.

"I'm bringing my cat, Elliot," said Edgar. Mr. Cummings wrote that down.

"I'm bringing my dog, Gladys," said Lenny when it was his turn. Gladys was Smiley's mother, but she wasn't much older than Smiley. Not like a regular mother.

Another boy said he was bringing a turtle. There were lots of turtles. And lots of gerbils.

Gus told about Smiley.

Then Mr. Cummings pointed at Punkin Head.

Poor Punkin Head, I thought. He's going to have to tell him he has no pet.

"I'm bringing my parrot," said Punkin Head. "He can talk. He can even spell."

You could have knocked me over with a feather, as my aunt Fluffy says. What was Punkin Head talking about?

But Mr. Cummings wrote it down and went on to the next person. Everyone was leaning over toward Punkin Head to ask about his parrot. Punkin Head was rattling off all kinds of stuff about him.

"It's green," I heard him say, "and it has this long red tail."

When everyone had told about what pet they were bringing, Mr. Cummings said, "Remember, there will be a blue ribbon for the winner. For the best pet in every category."

So there was a winner! Smiley would take first place.

"Whose room will the ribbon hang in?" asked Gus.

"We'll take turns," I said.

"What's a category?" said Lily. "If it's just a prize for cats, it's not fair."

"A category doesn't mean cats," roared Lenny Fox. "It means like a group. A prize for the best dog, the best cat, the best turtle."

When the meeting was over and school was out, I ran up to Punkin Head.

"When did you get a parrot?" I said. "Why didn't you tell me before?"

Punkin Head hung his head and kicked a rock in the snow. "I haven't got one yet," he admitted. "But I'm going to."

"You lied?" I said. "You lied to the principal?"

"Everyone else has a pet," Punkin

Head blurted out. "I didn't want to be the only one without a pet."

I could understand that. "But a *parrot*?" I said. "Why did you make up a parrot?"

"Anyone can have a dog or cat or gerbil or fish. I wanted something special."

I suppose if you make up a pet, you might as well make up a fancy one. It's no bigger lie to make up a parrot than to make up a fish.

"What are you going to do?" I demanded. I was getting heated up. Punkin Head was getting into another pickle. "Mr. Cummings has your name down for a parrot. A real parrot. A talking parrot."

"I'm going to get one," said my friend. "I've got money in my bank. I can go to the mall and get one. I saw them in the pet store. They've got a lot of them sitting on those sticks. When you come in, this yellow guy says, 'Hi, good-lookin'.' "

"Will your mom let you?" I asked. I had the feeling a lot of mothers might not like parrots talking to friends and relatives who came to visit. I'd seen a parrot on TV who said bad words.

"I'll keep it in my room," said Punkin Head. "She won't even know."

"I don't think you can keep a parrot a secret," I said.

"Then I'll keep him at your house," he said.

I held up my hand. It's easy enough to get in trouble without trying. I saw trouble here, ahead of time. "No way," I said. "Smiley might eat a parrot."

"Come to the mall with me," begged Punkin Head. "I'll go home and get my money and we'll go to the pet store."

"I suppose you'll need help getting him home," I said. "He'll have to be in a box or something, or he'll get sick. It's cold out and parrots are from somewhere hot by the equator."

"Meet you in ten minutes in front of Mrs. Hood's," said Punkin Head. Mrs. Hood is an old lady who lives on the edge of our development. When they put our condos in, she wouldn't sell her old farmhouse and barn, so it was stuck right on the edge of Huckleberry Heights. At Halloween we'd thought the barn was haunted, but we found out it wasn't.

Gus wanted to come when he heard about the parrot. Then we met Lily. She was sliding down her aunt's hill on her sled. Her aunt lives in our building. "Can I come?" she asked. "I love to go to the mall."

On the way to Mrs. Hood's, Lenny and Edgar joined us.

"Why didn't you bring the whole neighborhood," said Punkin Head sullenly. "Now everybody knows I haven't got a parrot."

"You will have one soon," I said. "It's hard to keep a secret in Huckleberry Heights."

"I think it's neat you're getting a parrot," said Lily.

"He'll win the prize," said Lenny.

We all tried to make Punkin Head feel important. It was the least we could do for a petless friend.

The snow had turned to slop outside,

and we slushed along kicking it at each other. By the time we got to the mall, we were all kind of wet. Our boots left muddy wet marks when we went into the mall and toward the pet store.

"Look!" shouted Edgar. "I can see your parrot from here!"

Sure enough, a big green parrot was sitting on a perch right inside the pet store door. He wasn't even in a cage!

"Come in, come in, come in!" said a voice.

We looked around for the man who was polite enough to invite us in. But it wasn't a man. It was Punkin Head's bird!

"Buy that one,"said Lily."It can really talk."

"Come in, come in, come in," the parrot repeated.

"I think that's all it can say," I said.

"Pardon me, but do you have any other parrots?" Punkin Head was asking the clerk. Good for Punkin Head. He wasn't going to take the first pet he saw. Punkin Head was a wise shopper.

"Over here," said the clerk. She led us to the side of the store where there was a row of sticks and cages.

"Wow!" said Lily. "You've got lots to choose from."

Punkin Head walked back and forth, back and forth, looking at them all closely.

"I say this blue one," said Lily. "Blue is my favorite color."

Gus liked the big yellow one that had a sign, POLLY, on her cage.

Lenny liked the one that was ringing its bell. "It's smarter than the others," he said.

It took Punkin Head a long time to decide. The rest of us got tired of parrots and walked around looking at dog and cat stuff. I saw a jacket for Smiley that would look good on him, but it cost thirty-nine dollars. "He's got a coat," said Gus. "A fur coat."

We went back to Punkin Head and told him to hurry up. "It will be dark by the time we get out of here," I said.

"I guess I'll take that one," said Punkin Head. "Even though it costs more than a lot of the others."

I looked at the price tags on the front of the cages. The one for the bird Punkin Head wanted looked like it said three dollars.

"That's a lot," said Punkin Head. "I won't have any money left to Christmas-shop. But it will be worth it."

We all agreed with him. This parrot was worth three dollars. Even if all it said was "Come in."

We all lined up at the counter. "I want that parrot," Punkin Head told the clerk. "It's going to be in a pet show. Can you wrap it up real good so it won't get a cold on the way home?"

The clerk had a funny look on her face. I don't know why. This was a pet store, wasn't it? Didn't they want to sell pets?

"Are you sure you want a parrot?" the clerk said.

"Perfectly sure," answered Lenny. "He wants a parrot that talks."

The clerk went in a back room and

came out with an older clerk.

"Will you be paying with cash, check, or credit card, young man?" he said.

I started to roar at the picture of Punkin Head with a credit card. Yeah, Punkin Head, take out your old checkbook and write a check. All this fuss over three dollars.

Punkin Head reached into his pocket and dragged out his three dollars all in nickels and dimes. And a few pennies.

"Money," he said. "I'll pay with money, out of my bank."

When all the money was on the counter, the clerks just stood there.

I wondered why they didn't wrap the bird up. Then I found out.

"This parrot is on sale today," said the clerk finally. "That's why it is up front. It is half price, three thousand dollars."

We all ran back to the parrot to look at the price tag.

"That says three dollars!" said Punkin Head. "A three and some zeros."

"There are lots of zeros," said Lily,
pointing.

I looked closely and counted three and
then the decimal point and two more
little ones.

"It's made to look like three dollars,
but it is really three thousand," said
Lenny. "I guess Punkin Head is two thousand, nine hundred and ninety-seven
dollars short."

"No bird could cost that much," said
Edgar. "Even if it was made out of gold.
Even if it had diamond eyes."

We went back to the other parrots to check their tags. They were even worse. As the man said, this one was on sale.

"I'm sorry," said the clerk. "Parrots are very expensive birds."

Punkin Head gathered up all his nickels and dimes and put them back into his pocket. I put my arm around his shoulder. I felt like saying "That's what you get for making up stories," but instead I said, "We'll find you another pet."

"I don't want another pet," wailed Punkin Head. "I have to get a parrot."

All of us sloshed home through the wet snow, thinking about his problem. I'd been sure we would be carrying a parrot cage on the way back. And we were empty-handed.

"What's the closest thing to a parrot?" I asked. "Maybe there is something that looks like a parrot."

"A canary," said Lily. "My aunt has a canary."

"Too small," said Lenny. "And too yellow."

"Parrots are big," said Edgar. "Like a chicken."

"Mrs. Hood has chickens," said Punkin Head.

Oh, no. I could see a light bulb turn on in Punkin Head's brain.

"A chicken is white," I said sensibly. "And they definitely don't talk. Nobody would think a white chicken was a talking parrot."

I laughed at the very thought of it. Punkin Head was talking like a crazed, desperate man. Parrot crazy.

"Unless," said Lenny, "there was a way of making its feathers green."

"Even if Mrs. Hood did lend us a chicken," I said, "she wouldn't want it returned to her all green."

"Food dye washes out," said Lily. "And it's harmless for children and pets. It says right on the bottle."

"The first rain would wash that chicken white again," said Edgar.

We were in front of my house now, and Marcy was calling me from the door. "Where were you so long? It's getting dark out."

53

"A chicken still doesn't talk," I said. "and it's too late now to do anything about it. Let's sleep on it."

Aunt Fluffy always said that. What she meant was that in the morning you would have forgotten about some silly idea that seemed real smart the night before. I was sure hoping that would happen when Punkin Head slept on it. That he'd get up in the morning and say, "What a dumb idea that was." I'd agree with him and say, "Maybe there's a place you can rent a pet, the way people rent a car."

But the next morning Punkin Head had not changed his mind. In fact, he had improved his idea, he said.

After school he rounded us all up in his garage, where he'd made a pen for the chicken/parrot. He had a dish full of leftover food and some sand for it to scratch in. "This is where Polly will live."

"What if it's a boy?" shrieked Edgar.

"It doesn't matter," said Punkin Head. "All parrots are called Polly."

54

He sure was ready for his new pet. All he had to do was get it.

"Will you guys come to Mrs. Hood's with me?" he begged.

I didn't feel like being any part of this dumb stunt, but we always stick together in Huckleberry Heights. I knew how important it was to Punkin Head to have a pet to enter in the pet show. A different pet than the others had. This one sure would be different.

Edgar looked doubtful. So did Lily.

But Lenny and I agreed to come with him to Mrs. Hood's, and Edgar and Lily didn't want to be left out. Neither did Gus.

"Why, here are all of my friends to visit me!" exclaimed Mrs. Hood when we knocked on her front door. Her dog, Rex, gave a big bark, but his tail was wagging.

"We came to borrow a chicken," said Punkin Head politely. "It's for a pet show."

Gus started to say he'd be made into a parrot, but Punkin Head stepped on his foot to keep him quiet.

Mrs. Hood laughed and said, "I thought you wanted one to roast for dinner." Then she told us we'd have to be careful, a chicken could peck us with its bill. We all agreed to be careful and ran out to the henhouse to find the right bird.

There were brown chickens and black ones and spotted ones, but mostly white ones.

"There it is!" pointed Punkin Head. "There's my parrot!"

Mrs. Hood came out with a sack to put it in, but Punkin Head wanted to walk it home on a leash. He tied a little string he brought to its leg.

"We'll take good care of it," said Punkin Head. "It might win a prize in the pet show."

"Give it plenty of water," said Mrs. Hood. "And here is a little bag of feed for its meals."

We waved good-bye to Mrs. Hood and started down Tiger Tail Trail walking a chicken called Polly through the snow. I hoped the big kids didn't see us. I'd be humiliated.

The chicken flapped and squawked and didn't want to walk on a leash. By the time we got to Punkin Head's garage, it had lost a few feathers.

"I brought some green food dye," said Lily. "My mom had lots left over from St. Patrick's Day. She made green cupcakes last year, with green jelly beans inside."

"What do we put the dye on it with?" asked Edgar.

"I think we need a paint brush, like we use in school," said Lenny.

Punkin Head ran to his room and got some brushes from his paint set.

"I'll hold Polly," said Lenny, "and you guys paint it."

Lily dipped the brush in the dye and began to paint the wings. I did the top of its head and its chest. Punkin Head found some red dye in his mother's cupboard and painted the tail red.

Polly did not want to be painted. It did not want to be a parrot. It flapped and sputtered. The more it flapped, the more paint splattered onto Lenny.

"Hey, you guys, hurry up! I'm greener than Polly is."

We tried to hurry, but it wasn't easy painting a chicken. We used all the dye in the bottles, and at last it was green and red.

"Christmas colors!" I said. "It's a Christmas parrot!"

"You better be sure it stays in the garage, Punkin Head," I said. "If it gets out in the snow, its color will wash off."

"I will," said Punkin Head. "No one comes out here, it'll be fine. My dad parks the car on the street."

The chicken pecked at its food and drank some water.

"I'm going to train it to sit on my shoulder," said Punkin Head. "That's what parrots do in movies. They sit on their owner's shoulder."

"You need a patch over your eye," said Edgar. "Guys who have parrots have a patch on one eye and a wooden leg."

I thought that was carrying things too far.

"You don't need to worry about a wooden leg," I said. "The problem I see is that people at the pet show are going to expect a parrot to talk. And a chicken simply doesn't talk. Even if it's green."

"Ho," said Punkin Head, waving my problem away. "I already thought of that. This parrot is going to talk, all right, and I know just how we're going to do it."

6

I didn't like the sound of that *we*. I didn't have an idea in my head about how to get a chicken to talk. And in less than a week. Even if we got some chicken expert in from another state, he couldn't do it in a week.

"It's simple," said Punkin Head. "I'll be on the stage in the auditorium with Polly on my shoulder, and I'll ask it questions. And one of you will be behind the curtain where no one can see you, and you'll answer. You'll be the parrot. You know, like a ventriloquist. Like the Muppets."

"Wow," said Lenny.

"Who is going to be the parrot?" asked Edgar suspiciously.

"Not me," I said.

"Come on," said Punkin Head. "You'd be best at it."

"I'll be the parrot," said Gus, jumping up and down.

But Punkin Head didn't pay any attention to him. He had me in mind for the job.

"Tony is good at stuff," he said.

Lenny and Edgar and Lily quickly agreed. "He's smart," said Lenny with admiration.

"And trustworthy," said Lily.

What kind of compliments were these? All tricks to get me to do this dirty job. The job no one else wanted. If someone got caught behind the curtain, it would be me. If someone pulled the curtain aside and the whole audience saw me make a fool of myself pretending to be a parrot, I'd be the laughingstock of Huckleberry Heights.

"I'll do it," Gus piped up again.

"We'll have to rehearse," said Punkin Head, still ignoring my little brother. I admit, Gus isn't as mature or dependable as I am.

"I can't rehearse," I said. "I have to get Smiley ready for the show, and make a holiday gift, and I have to read *A Christmas Carol*."

Punkin Head looked disappointed. So did my other friends. Punkin Head gave his sob story to Marcy and Daisy and George Nelson when they came by, and even Marcy started making me feel guilty.

"Help him out, Tony," she said. "Poor Punkin Head, he hasn't even got a pet of his own."

I was surprised at Marcy. She should have seen how dumb this whole idea was. Probably she wanted me to look bad onstage.

"Be a parrot," said Daisy. "He needs you."

What could I do? "All right," I said. "But it isn't going to work."

The next morning Miss Roscoe said, "I hope you are all getting your pets spruced up for the pet contest! It's next Saturday and it's coming fast."

Punkin Head's chicken was spruced up, all right.

"How many have read *A Christmas Carol*?" asked Miss Roscoe.

A few hands went up, but wavered.

"Today we are going to choose parts." Miss Roscoe put the names of the characters on the board. She told us a bit about each one: that Tiny Tim limped. And Scrooge hated Christmas. And old Marley was dead. And Bob Cratchit was poor as a church mouse. There weren't many parts for girls, so the girls had to play boys.

"I think Lily would be a very nice Tiny Tim," said Miss Roscoe. "Tiny Tim had long hair and curls."

Everyone clapped and Lily bowed. She wanted to be Tiny Tim!

"Who do you think would make a good Scrooge?" asked Miss Roscoe. "His is the lead part."

Everyone in the room pointed to me.

"Tony!" shouted Edgar. "He's the best actor in the room."

"Congratulations, Tony! Your fans have spoken."

Through no choice of my own, I was

slated to go onstage twice in one month. What was it about me that got me into these things? I was a pushover, that's what it was.

"It's because you're so popular," said my mother that evening when I told her.

"You are kind and friendly," said my aunt Fluffy, who was at our house making Christmas cookies with my mom. "Everyone likes you."

"Especially the girls," said Gus, sampling the dough.

Gus was right, girls did like me. Especially Lily. And this fall an older girl in Marcy's grade named Tara liked me. Maybe it was my fate.

Scrooge had a lot of lines to say, even though Miss Roscoe had shortened the play a lot and made it kind of simple.

"You're a grouch," laughed Lily, poking me in the ribs. "You hate Christmas."

When we started practicing, all the kids in the room called me Scrooge.

On Wednesday Miss Roscoe held up an old hat.

"Maybe she's going to pull a rabbit out of it!" said Lily.

But what she pulled out was not a rabbit. It was a handful of names. "These," she said, "will tell you who your special holiday friend is. Whom your gift will be for."

"Is it a secret?" called out Lucas. "Is our special holiday friend a secret?"

Miss Roscoe nodded. "I think it will be more fun if we don't tell until the party."

She walked up and down the aisle, and we all drew names. I was almost the last one to draw. I drew Lily's name.

I knew it! I thought. All the people in the room and I drew my own girlfriend. I'd probably give her a present anyway. I like Lily well enough, but I was feeling pressured. Lily in my room, Lily in the play with me, Lily my special holiday friend, Lily living almost next door to me. There was just too much Lily. And Lily would read a lot into my drawing her name. She'd say it was fate. She believed in those spooky things, like fortune-tellers. At this rate we'd end up married before we got to high school. A child groom. I felt trapped. I was too young to go steady.

I sat and wondered what I could make for Lily that she'd like but wouldn't be romantic. She made everything seem romantic.

At recess she said, "You drew my name, didn't you? I know you did. I can see it on your face!"

I told you she was spooky. She read my mind.

"You did you did you did!" she said, running around the playground telling everyone.

"What are you going to get Lily?" said Lenny, coming up to me before the bell rang.

"I don't know yet," I said.

After school I went home and made a list of what I had to do before Christmas. 1. Christmas-shop for my family. 2. Make Lily's present. 3. Learn my lines for the play. 4. Finish *A Christmas Carol*. 5. Practice being a parrot. 6. Get Smiley ready for Saturday.

Miss Roscoe said the holidays were a time to have a lot of fun. But right now it looked as if I wouldn't have much time to have fun. I had to do the things on my list. I took my pencil and wrote: *number 7: Have fun*. I'd have to work it in somehow.

I put my list up on my bulletin board. "I'll check off everything as I do it," I said out loud.

"Anthony," my mother called from downstairs. "Can you come down here a minute please?"

Her voice had that edge to it that was overly sweet. The voice she uses when we have company, or when someone besides the family is in the house. I wondered what stranger was in our living room.

"Coming," I called. I forgot about my list and put my head around the corner of the stairs. I could see Aunt Fluffy standing there with a big smile on her face. I wondered why my mom had her company voice on when there was no company, only Aunt Fluffy, her own sister.

I went down the steps two at a time and landed at my aunt's feet. Then I knew why Mom had talked like that. Just inside the door in the spot she calls the foyer, stood a strange man. A tall man with sunglasses on even though it was winter.

"I want you to meet Miles Swann," said my mother. "Mr. Swann, this is my oldest son, Anthony."

"Hello," I said, reaching out my hand to meet his.

Maybe this was the man who was coming to fix the dishwasher. But usually my mom doesn't call me downstairs to shake the hands of repairmen.

Aunt Fluffy turned pink and reached out her hand and put it into Mr. Swann's. "This is my friend, Anthony. My new friend, Miles."

I put her words together with her pink, smiley face and it dawned on me. This was my aunt's boyfriend. A boyfriend she liked well enough to bring over to meet the family. Would I be bringing Lily around to meet Marcy's children some winter day in the future?

I should have felt happy about Aunt Fluffy's new friend. Instead I felt jealous. Aunt Fluffy was ours. She was at our house as much as she was home. Lately she hadn't been, and now I knew why.

"We're on the way up north to ski," said Aunt Fluffy. "For the weekend."

My aunt always told me she was going to take me to the slopes. She said we'd stay in one of those little cabins in Lutsen and drink cider around a fire in the lodge. Now this guy who none of us knew very well was going instead.

"I have a little daughter about your age," said Mr. Swann.

"I can't wait till you all meet her," Aunt Fluffy gushed. "You'll love Rosalie. You'll see her Christmas Eve."

I thought of the list on my bulletin board. I'd have to go up and cross something off. Number 7.

7

"**Y**ou won't be at our pet show on Saturday," I said. "You'll miss seeing Smiley win a blue ribbon."

"I hate to miss that," said my aunt Fluffy cheerfully. It didn't look like she was too torn up with grief. "I'll see the blue ribbon when I get back."

Saturday came fast. Miss Roscoe was right. The holidays were here before we knew it. And instead of our regular Christmas with our loved ones, we had to have a total stranger sitting by the tree, making our aunt all dizzy-looking. She always gave a lot of thought to our gifts—this year she'd be thinking about gifts for Miles and Rosalie. And how could we act crazy the way we always did, when there were strangers in the house?

"I don't think we should have strangers on Christmas," I told my mom.

"Why, Anthony, that's what Christmas is all about! Sharing and bringing new people into our lives. Making new friends."

It didn't feel that way to me. It felt like just one more problem to add to my list.

"Marcella and Fergus can't wait to expand our little family. To welcome little Rosalie into our circle."

Good for them. That's because they don't have this sense of foreboding that I do. They just go along being happy about stuff and not even knowing something awful could happen any minute. I'm blessed with this sort of gift for seeking out disaster. They don't have it.

On Saturday, Smiley was brushed so he shone like tinsel. No mats. His hair was like silk. I forgot to get ribbons for his ears, but Marcy tied one of her blue hair ribbons around his neck. He even smelled good. I put some of my mom's Eternity on him.

My mom drove us so Smiley wouldn't get his feet wet. We picked up Lily and her fuzzy cat. It looked like a giant bedroom slipper, it was so clean and puffy. Lenny and Gladys were on the corner, so we gave them a ride too. Edgar walked, with Elliot.

"It's snowing," whispered Lily in my ear in the backseat. "You know what that could mean."

"What?" I asked. I thought it might be one of those mushy messages.

"It means," she whispered, "that Punkin Head's parrot could turn back into a chicken. Its green will wash off."

"I hope he covered it," I said.

I was glad we didn't meet Punkin Head along the way. My mom would have stopped to give him a ride, and there were bound to have been questions. Not only that, but one car isn't big enough for two dogs, a cat, and a chicken.

When we arrived, Punkin Head was waiting.

"What do you suppose Punkin Head has under that brown bag?" asked my mother. "It seems to be very active."

"Just a pet," I said. I tried to act as if it was a normal thing to keep a pet in a brown bag.

"To keep it warm," added Lenny.

We jumped out of the car with our pets and dashed into the auditorium.

"We'll be there in half an hour," called my mom. I knew she'd be in the front row with Marcy and Daisy and George and their parents. It made me nervous thinking about it.

"All right!" said Mr. Cummings when we came in. "Line up back here with your pets."

I never saw so many animals in one place except the zoo. There were hamsters and goldfish and huge dogs and teensy little dogs and cats both fluffy and plain. There were a couple of snakes and a newt and a lot of turtles. But there was only one parrot/chicken combination. It sounded like a circus in there. There was growling and hissing and screaming and yelling, and in five minutes a wiry fox terrier starting picking on Smiley. Smiley growled and chased him around the auditorium, and Mr. Cummings said I had to keep Smiley on a leash.

"All owners must stay in control of their animals," he was saying into the microphone.

Microphones scare Smiley, and he began to howl his wolf howl. Mr. Cummings was getting very red in the face. He looked as if this pet show was something he wished he had not started.

"I'll bet he didn't think there would be this many pets," yelled Edgar over the din. "A lot of kids brought two or three of them. He bit off more than he could chew."

Mr. Cummings called in help. Two eighth-grade boys were grouping the dog and cat sections according to small, medium, and large. They were also grouping the cats into fluffy and plain.

Lenny was brushing Gladys. Then he reached into a bag and took out, of all things, a Santa Claus costume.

"Why are you going to wear a costume?" I asked. "It's a pet show, not an owners' show."

"It's for Gladys," said Lenny, pulling the dog's legs through the red pants. He adjusted Gladys's tail so it came through a little hole in back. He pulled the top half over her head, and fastened a black belt around her waist. Gladys just sat still and let Lenny dress her.

"Smiley would have a fit!" said Gus. "He wouldn't wear any old suit that people laugh at."

"That's why he won't win," said Lenny. Lenny is a real businessman.

"That's not fair!" I shouted. "No one said to dress the animals in costumes."

"You have to use your head," said Lenny, pointing to his forehead. "You have to be creative."

Lenny was putting four black boots on his pet's feet. Then he put a hat on Gladys's head with an elastic that went

under her chin so when she walked, it wouldn't fall off.

"Sit up!" called Lenny.

Gladys did. What a clown. Smiley would be embarrassed to do that. Sit up in a Santa Claus suit.

Smiley had one paw on Mr. Cummings's knee. He had his head cocked to the side the cute way he does. My mom says it makes him very lovable. Before I could pull him away, he licked Mr. Cummings's hand.

I yanked Smiley back. At this rate he'd be out of the show for slobbering all over the judge. There's probably a rule about slobbering all over judges, especially when the judge is your principal.

Mr. Cummings walked over to Punkin Head. I heard him ask some questions. Then he threw his head back and laughed loudly. He put Punkin Head and his parrot in a separate category, although there were a couple of parakeets nearby.

Punkin Head was motioning me over to him. "Quick!" he was saying.

I put Gus in charge of Smiley and walked over to Punkin Head. "Stay near me. Get behind that curtain," he said. "Mr. Cummings laughed at Polly. I don't think he believed he was a real parrot because he couldn't talk. If you'd have been here, he'd have believed me."

"I don't want to go back there yet! I'll miss seeing the show. I'll miss seeing Smiley win a blue ribbon."

But Punkin Head was pushing me. I gave him a punch back, and Miss Roscoe gave me one of those looks to watch out. I didn't want to start a fight onstage, so I got back of the curtain. Not only would I miss the show, but I'd probably be found out and be the laughingstock of Huckleberry Heights. I wondered if I would even be disqualified for impersonating a parrot.

"I'll get you for this, Punkin Head," I snorted.

The main curtain opened, I could tell by the applause. One by one the kids brought out their pets and showed what they could do. I tried to peek through the curtain, but Punkin Head was watching and pulled it back over my face to keep me hidden.

The cats took a long time. I heard Lily's voice saying how her cat could dust the furniture with his tail, but he wouldn't do it in public. People clapped for her.

All Lenny had to do was walk onstage with Gladys and it brought the house down. She didn't even have to do any tricks. I didn't know which dog was Smiley because I didn't hear Gus's voice.

"Okay!" whispered Punkin Head. "Parrots are next!"

"The next category," Mr. Cummings was saying, "is—parrots! And we have one entry by young Mr. Maloney."

"This is my talking parrot," I heard Punkin Head say. "He is from South America and costs lots of money. Say your name for the audience, Polly."

This was my cue. "My name is Polly," I said in my parrot voice. I felt like an idiot. "Polly wants a cracker."

"How old are you?" asked Punkin Head.

"Four," I said.

"Sing a song for us," I heard Punkin Head say.

Sing? What was Punkin Head thinking of? I never agreed to sing. I said I'd answer two questions and that was it.

"Sing," repeated Punkin Head. The crowd applauded. They clapped in rhythm, as if urging Polly to sing. I knew what was the matter. Punkin Head was loving the applause. He didn't want to stop! He was a ham!

"Sing 'God Bless America,' " said Punkin Head.

I was humiliated. But I sang the first verse and the audience was hooting and hollering. I heard a little girl yell, "Mama, that chicken *talks*! Just like Big Bird!"

"Big Bird is yellow," shouted Punkin Head to the little girl. "This isn't a chicken, it's a green parrot."

"Say a poem," Punkin Head ordered me now.

A poem? Two could play at this game. I'd say a poem all right.

"Punkin Head's a dunderhead,
He really thinks he's funny.
If he wants me to talk some more
He'll have to pay me money."

Everyone screamed laughing except Punkin Head. I just had to see what was going on. Why should Punkin Head get all the attention and have all the fun? I was doing the work. I pulled the curtain back and people were on their feet whistling and stamping.

Punkin Head gave me a kick backward with his foot. "That poem wasn't funny," he whispered.

"Then why are they all laughing?" I asked.

Mr. Cummings had to hold up his hand for silence. He came up onstage with tears running down his face and pulled the curtain back, just as I thought he would. I was about to be disqualified. Or expelled from school. Or both.

He led me out onto the stage next to Punkin Head and his green chicken.

"And here we have our parrot's voice," Mr. Cummings said, pointing to me.

"I didn't want to—" I started. But before I could finish, the principal was saying something about the most entertaining act he'd ever seen and what a clever team we were to think of this.

"It was the highlight of the show," said Mr. Cummings. "This chick-ot, or pare-ken, is the winner in its category!"

Mr. Cummings slapped a blue ribbon on Punkin Head's chest because the chicken wouldn't hold still long enough to have it stick to his feathers.

"And another blue ribbon for Anthony Doyle, the winner in a very special new category: the voice of a parrot, and a wonderful actor!"

Well, you should have heard that crowd clap. I was mad my aunt wasn't there to see how funny I was. But that's show biz.

The rest of the show was pretty boring. Parakeets and snakes weren't funny at all.

"Great going!" said Daisy Otis when it was over.

"You were so cute!" said my ex-girlfriend, Tara.

"I told you the parrot was a great idea," said Punkin Head.

We all had to admit, Punkin Head was right for once.

"Didn't Smiley win anything?" I asked Gus.

Gus shook his head. "Gladys won the blue ribbon in the dog category," he said. "People clapped the most when she came out dressed like Santa Claus."

Well, I suppose if Smiley couldn't win, the next best thing was having his mother be a prizewinner.

"I get my dog all spiffed up for a contest, and he loses," I said to my friends. "And I talk for a chicken and win a blue ribbon."

"All's well that ends well," said my mother, giving me a hug.

We all piled into the car and drove home. I ran right to my room and did two things. I hung my blue ribbon on my wall, and I took out my list and a pencil and put a heavy dark line through number 5, number 6, and number 7.

The pet show was over, I had said my lines, and I had to admit I had fun. There's no fun more fun than being the star of a show. Even when you didn't want to be in it.

8

In the afternoon we carefully washed Polly in Punkin Head's laundry tub and dried him. Then we took him back to Mrs. Hood and put him in the pen with the other chickens.

"He'll think he's too good to be in a barnyard," Mrs. Hood said, laughing, when she'd heard the story. "He's a show business chicken."

Mrs. Hood was making fudge in her big warm kitchen, and she asked us in to have some.

"How do you get it to stay together?" asked Gus. "Our fudge ran all over the place."

"You need a candy thermometer," said

our friend. She held up something like the doctor puts in my mouth when I'm sick, only bigger. "It has to be just the right temperature."

After we left Mrs. Hood's, I went home and finished reading *A Christmas Carol.* I checked it off my list. Christmas was a lot of work and it was just starting. This next week was the last week of school before vacation. On Friday was the play and the party, and I'd have to come up with Lily's homemade gift.

"We're having a Christmas party in our room," said Gus the next morning. "We're having a tree and presents and a lot of stuff to eat."

"Everyone has a party," said Marcy. "We're having a Hanukkah party too."

"We have to make a gift," I said at breakfast. "We can't buy one."

"I think all of our gifts should be homemade," said my mother cheerfully. "That way it shows there is love in it."

I don't know how much love is in a toilet-paper holder in the shape of a dog's head. That's what Edgar was making for the person whose name he drew. I sure hoped I wasn't that person.

"After we do the dishes, we'll clear the table and get to work creating things our friends will like."

Gus was wild about this idea. He loved to make a mess. The stickier and gooier, the better.

My mom got out paper and scissors and glue and string and bits of wood and old cereal cartons. It reminded me more of Cub Scouts than of Christmas.

"I can't give Lily any old cereal box," I cried. I may not want to get married yet, but I sure didn't want to lose my girlfriend.

"I have an idea," said my mother.

Marcy groaned. My mom's ideas could be fatal.

My mom went down to the basement, and when she came up she was carrying a box of faucet parts. Screws and washers and short copper pipes and handles that said Hot or Cold. We had a sculpture in our living room made out of old pipes and faucets from her faucet company. "Waste not, want not" was her motto.

"Not more faucet paperweights," said Marcy. "Aunt Fluffy has them all over her house."

"A person can't have too many paperweights," said my mother. "But no, we are not making paperweights. I have a better idea. A new idea. We are going to make jewelry."

She held up a little swirl of copper wire. "I see beauty in metal," she said. "We can cut and bend in any way the muse moves us. No one in the world will have a pair of earrings like the ones you make. No one will have to take them back to the store to exchange and say, 'I got two pairs just like this.' Think of that, children."

"I got Douglas's name," whined Gus. "Douglas doesn't wear earrings."

"We'll make him a tie clasp," said our mother.

"He doesn't wear ties," said Gus.

"He will someday, and he'll be very grateful."

We sat and looked at the pipes, and eventually we got in the mood. I made Lily a bracelet out of washers. My mom held it up to the light and said, "Just look at that shine!"

I wondered if I should make her a ring to match. Then she'd probably yell all over the playground that we were engaged. I decided the bracelet was enough.

In the middle of this mess, Lenny came by and pitched in making earrings for his mother.

"I think I'd like to go into this business, Mrs. Doyle," he said. "A person could have an assembly line and sell this stuff."

"Mass production is not creative, Leonard," said my mother.

"But it pays well," said my friend.

By suppertime we were all wearing faucet, wire, or pipe jewelry, even Smiley. My mom got little boxes out and we wrapped the stuff and put names on it. I was starting to get the Christmas spirit.

"I hope we get other stuff besides this for Christmas," said Gus.

"Wait and see," sang our mother.

At suppertime my mom pushed all the stuff aside and made some good bacon, lettuce, and tomato sandwiches, and we opened cans of soup. Lenny stayed. Just as we dug into our soup there was a rap on the door.

"Merry Merry Huckleberry!" boomed a voice. I could smell the smell of pine. Like a woods. "We were just out cutting down our Christmas tree," said Mr. Otis, "and we thought maybe you'd like a fresh tree too."

"It's lovely!" exclaimed my mother. "Come in and have supper with us."

So Mr. Otis set this eight-foot tree up next to the fireplace, and he and Mrs. Otis and Daisy all trooped in for supper.

The whole house smelled like Christmas.

"Even without decorations, it's beautiful," said Marcy. "I think we should sing Christmas songs."

We did. All of us. Here I was, having

fun in spite of myself. And the best part was, I got to cross something else off my list. I had Lily's present made.

Marcy and Daisy planned their vacation shopping trip to the mall, and Lenny and I and Gus made some new Christmas tree ornaments from pipes and nuts and bolts. We painted them bright colors.

"It's too bad Aunt Fluffy and Giles aren't here with us," said my mother.

"Miles," said Marcy. "His name is Miles."

Why did my mother have to bring that up now? It was the last cloud hanging over my holidays—that and playing Scrooge in the school play. I had this awful feeling that I had lost my aunt, my dear aunt Fluffy, to people who would take her away from us. Miles and Rosalie didn't deserve her. She was ours. And maybe Marcy and Gus and I would have to fight for her.

9

"We have to get rid of Miles and Rosalie," I said to Marcy and Gus on Monday morning.

You'd think I'd said something terrible. Marcy looked shocked.

"What do you mean, 'rid of'?" she asked.

"Not around Aunt Fluffy."

"Aunt Fluffy likes them," said Marcy. "They make her happy. Why would we want them to leave?"

"She's our aunt," I shouted. "These people aren't even any relation!"

"They will be when they get married!" piped Gus. "Miles will be our uncle and Rosalie will be our cousin! Mom said so."

There was that word *marry* again. Is there some conspiracy in our family that everyone has to get married?

"Tony, Fluffy needs to have a boyfriend. People need—partners. She'd be lonely."

"She has us," I yelled.

"That's different," said Marcy. Then she launched into this thing that was right on the edge of the facts of life. "It's nature," she ended up. "We can't interfere with nature. Anyway, it's Christmas, and who wants to do a nasty thing like that at Christmas? We are supposed to be happy and have fun during the holidays."

Where had I heard that before? I went out and slammed the door. On the way to school I said to my friends, "I don't like my aunt's boyfriend and little girl. I want to do something so they'll leave Aunt Fluffy alone."

It sounded mean even as I said it. Even to me. I didn't even *know* his little girl.

"Does she like this guy?" asked Lenny.

I nodded.

"Then they should be together," he said. "Grown-ups like to be with other people."

I held up my hand. I didn't want another lecture.

"I know how you can get rid of them," whispered Punkin Head.

At last, a sympathetic soul. Punkin Head was great at schemes. I needed a good schemer.

"You put this pail of water on a shelf over the door," he confided. "Then you tie a string from the pail to the doorknob. When this guy Piles comes in, swooosh, he's swimming. I think he'll get the idea."

"Miles," I said. "His name is Miles. And that's the oldest trick in the book. Last time we did it, the water spilled on me."

But now Punkin Head was off with Gus, swinging on the jungle gym on the playground.

"Give it up," said Edgar.

"Love is beautiful," said Lily, sidling up to me. "I'll bet they get married."

I didn't have any more time that week to dwell on schemes. I was too busy getting ready to say "Bah, humbug," in our play. I was this crabby old guy who hated Christmas. Not only that, I was selfish and mean and didn't pay Bob Cratchit enough money to buy food for his family. And poor Tiny Tim had a limp.

"You see what a miserable man Scrooge was," said Miss Roscoe one afternoon. "He didn't have the Christmas spirit at all."

I started feeling good about playing this character. I loved being a mean and crabby person onstage. I yelled "Bah, humbug" louder than I needed to, Miss Roscoe said. But it wasn't until Friday when we gave the play that it came to me. Right there onstage, with Lily dressed up as Tiny Tim, and old Marley dragging his chains. The reason I liked being the mean, selfish guy in the play was that he was just like me. I was Scrooge! I had no Christmas spirit either!

After the play, the applause was thunderous. "Tony really put his heart and soul into his acting," said Miss Roscoe.

No, I didn't, I thought. I was a natural. I was born for the part. I was going to be a Scrooge when I grew up, and everyone would hate me. I'd end up in a cold little hut with a candle burning instead of a fire and no friends and everyone would be afraid of me!

I ate a lot of candy at the party, but my heart wasn't in it.

"I have to change," I said out loud to myself. Scrooge changed at the end of the play. Maybe it wasn't too late. To start with, I'd make a nice present for Miles and Rosalie. I'd make them feel welcome.

"Now it's time to open the gifts from our special person," called Miss Roscoe. We all gathered around the Christmas tree, and she called out the names.

"Oh, Tony!" screamed Lily when she opened her gift from me. "Did you make this yourself?" She fondled my washers and held them up to the light.

"All by myself," I said proudly.

"Anthony has talent in both acting and art," said Miss Roscoe.

"Thank you," I said.

Then Lily threw her arms around my neck and gave me a *kiss*. Right on my MOUTH, for Pete's sake.

It felt good. I almost threw my arms around her neck and kissed her back. Maybe there was more to this love and romance than I knew.

Then I opened my gift.

"Are you surprised? Are you surprised?" shouted Edgar as I held up the toilet-paper holder with the dog's face on it.

"Yes," I managed to say. "I didn't know you drew my name. It's very creative."

"Edgar is talented too!" said Miss Roscoe.

I didn't think it took talent to make a toilet-paper holder, but I didn't say it because I was trying to get over my negative attitude, my Scroogelike personality. I wanted to have the Christmas spirit.

When all the presents were opened, we sang holiday songs while Miss Roscoe played the piano. I was so full of Christmas spirit, I could hardly contain myself. And besides, this was the last day of school. We were just about on vacation!

On the way home Lily showed off her bracelet and I put Edgar's toilet-paper dog on my head.

That night we trimmed the tree Mr. Otis had brought us. We hung our homemade ornaments on the branches and some others too. My mom made popcorn balls, and the house smelled so good. Just about everything on my list was crossed off now, and I was free just to have fun, and think of some great gift for Miles and Rosalie. And for Marcy and Gus and my mom too.

I took a warm bath and put on my pajamas and crawled into bed. They were playing carols on my little radio.

"Tony?" said Marcy, at my door. She came in and sat on my bed.

"Maybe you're right about Miles. It

will change things. Maybe Aunt Fluffy is making a mistake, I mean, we don't know anything about this guy. And she'll fuss all over this Rosalie and we'll have to have real good manners and be polite even if she's a real pest."

I was really glad I didn't have Marcy's negative feelings.

"You have an attitude problem," I said. "I think it's good for Aunt Fluffy to have a boyfriend. And Christmas is the time to share and bring new love into our lives."

I sounded like a preacher, for heaven's sake.

"I thought you hated Miles!" said Marcy, punching me on the arm.

"Hate is a strong word," I said wisely. "That's the way Scrooge was, and look what happened to him."

Marcy looked at me suspiciously. She went out and shut my door. I started to laugh and laugh into my pillow. I couldn't stop. It was such fun confusing my sister. And it was fun not being Scrooge anymore.

10

Three days before Christmas we all went to the mall to get holiday gifts. I picked something out for Miles that I knew he'd like. A pair of ski gloves. And I got Rosalie a little pair of snowflake earrings. That took most of my money, but it would be worth it to make Aunt Fluffy happy. I got some crayons for Gus and eye shadow for Marcy. I don't think she had any this color orange. I got my mom a new pliers. She loves tools.

When we got home, I went to my room and wrapped them. Rosalie and Miles kept coming to my mind. I played the game I usually play. What's the

worst that could happen? Rosalie could be a little brat. A pest. Spoiled. Mean. Homely, with braces and an underbite. Hateful, tattletale. Well, I could deal with that. She might get the Christmas spirit too. If not, I could lend her *A Christmas Carol*.

On the other hand, she might be wonderful. Someone confident but not cocky. She might love to ride bikes and play ball.

Well, I'd find out soon enough. It was almost Christmas Eve.

My mom was really busy during the holidays. She gave a Christmas party at the office for all her faucet workers. And she had to work late because, believe this if you can, people bought more faucets around the holidays. "Happy Hanukkah, Merry Christmas, have a faucet!" some people must say.

Anyway, on Christmas Eve morning my mother was rattled. She was busy making these little hors d'oeuvres out of shrimp, when the phone rang and she got called into work.

"Anthony," she said, hanging up her apron on the back of the kitchen door, "I haven't wrapped Marcella's and Fergus's packages yet. Could you help me out with that? There's paper in the desk drawer."

"Sure," I said. "Where are they?"

"Marcy's are in my bottom drawer, and Fergus's are in my closet. Two big boxes for Fergus and three smaller ones for Marcy. Be sure you don't let them see you."

Her voice was already fading as she dashed out the door and started the car. "Thank you, dear!" she said. "That will be such a big help."

It made me feel good to do something useful. I hated to just sit around and watch the clock go toward Christmas Eve night. I dashed into my mother's room and shut the door. I got the wrapping paper out, and the red bows and tags. I wrote the tags out first. *To Marcella from Mother*. Then I wrote *To Fergus from Mother* on some with candy canes on them. Gus liked candy canes.

The next step was harder. I found the bottom drawer. But *which* bottom drawer? She must mean the drawer in her highboy. I pulled it out and there were three boxes. Smallish boxes. I really wanted to know what Marcy was getting, but I didn't think it would be right to snoop. I wanted to be surprised along with Marcy.

When I was through, the packages were beautiful. I slipped the cards under the bow and set them under our tree when no one was looking.

I opened my mom's closet and got a chair to reach the shelf. There were two boxes right in front. Biggish, just like my mom said. I cut paper just the right size so it didn't make a big lump, and taped it neatly. I chose paper with Santa Claus all over it. Gus loves Santa Clauses.

I put Gus's gifts from my mom in back of the tree, where he wouldn't see them right off and start to poke. Then I went and got my own gifts for everyone and put them out too. By noon, Marcy and Gus had theirs wrapped and under

the tree, and it drove us crazy waiting for Mom to come home. Gus's packages were lumpy and sticky and funny shapes, but I was dying to know what was in them.

About three o'clock it began to snow. Just a few lazy flakes drifting down.

"It's going to be a white Christmas," said Marcy.

"A whiter one, you mean," I said. "There already are piles of snow on the ground."

The guys stopped over with presents. Lenny brought me a model rocket and some Norwegian cookies his mom had made. I gave him a race car with stripes I made myself. Punkin Head brought me half of a candy bar.

About four o'clock my mom burst in the door. "I have some bad news," she said.

Bad news on Christmas Eve? With all our presents under the tree?

"Miles and Rosalie can't come," she said.

My first feeling was "Good!" but then

I remembered my Christmas spirit and the gifts we had ready for them. I was dying to meet this Rosalie on top of it. And what kind of a Christmas would it be with only us here?

"Miles's mother called him and she isn't well, so Miles felt they should spend the time with her. And she lives way up in Duluth. Aunt Fluffy said she hated to tell us at the last moment, but it couldn't be helped."

"Well, Aunt Fluffy will be here anyway," I said.

My mom shook her head. "She's going along with them," she said. "They had planned to be together for the holidays, and she didn't want to let Miles down just because they couldn't come here. Aunt Fluffy said they would come next weekend and celebrate Christmas on New Year's."

But what about now? I thought.

Marcy and Gus whined. It would take a lot of Christmas spirit to lift us now.

"We'll be all alone. One of those

families with no friends and relatives," moaned Marcy.

"We have friends," said my mother. "And it just happens that our relatives don't live in St. Paul."

Maybe I was being punished for wanting Aunt Fluffy to ourselves. We all got ready for Christmas Eve, and lit candles and put on clean clothes, and my mom had her red-and-green earrings on and she turned the lights on the tree and Gus started jumping around with excitement the way he always does, but there was something missing. What we needed (just as my mom told us) were strangers. Not *total* strangers, but someone to share with.

"We can't open presents this early," said my mom.

"We can play Scrabble," said Gus.

"We can play Scrabble any night," I said. "I don't want to play a game on Christmas Eve."

All of a sudden there was a knock on the door. Smiley began to bark and shake the sleighbells attached to his collar.

"Maybe Miles's mother got better," I said.

But it was Mr. Otis, from next door. "Ho ho ho," he shouted. "Merry Christmas! We thought we'd go caroling for a while, the Foxes, and Maloneys and Camps and anyone else who can make it. Can you join us?"

We had our jackets and boots on before you could say Huckleberry Heights. Smiley came too. We sang and sang and the snow was falling and the lights twinkled in everyone's windows and at every place we sang we had something to eat. At Lily's we had cranberry punch.

"Do you know what this is?" she said, pointing to a weed hanging from a string in her living room.

I shook my head.

"It's mistletoe," she said. "When someone stands under it, they get kissed."

"Really?" I said. "By who?"

"By me."

I stood under the weed. Sure enough, Lily was right. I did get kissed. For the second time this month by a girl.

I began to understand why Aunt Fluffy would rather be with Miles than with us. No doubt she knew about this mistletoe thing too.

I had more cranberry punch and then we went to Lenny's for hot soup and Edgar's for cocoa and marshmallows, and when we got to our house everyone piled in for my mom's shrimp hors d'oeuvres. The kids went down to our basement so we could holler and play without knocking the tree over. Everyone left just before midnight.

"Merry Merry Huckleberry!" called Mr. Otis, and we all called, "The same to you!"

"Now we can open our presents!" yelled Gus.

We all gathered around the tree. It didn't feel a bit lonely anymore. It's wonderful what a stranger or two will do for Christmas.

I opened a present from my mom. It was new saddlebags for my bike. I needed those. "Thanks!" I said, giving her a hug.

Gus had made me a tie holder. "I don't wear ties," I said. "I don't have any."

Gus's face fell. "But I can hang my belt on it," I said.

It was funny how even homemade gifts like this tie-holder thing looked really good under the tree lights.

Marcy opened one of the gifts from my mom that I had wrapped so well. She tore into that paper like crazy. She lifted the lid on the box.

"I hope you like it," said my mother. "I went to four stores looking for just the right one."

Marcy looked in the box. She didn't say anything.

"Well?" said our mother.

Marcy held up the present. It looked like a little bottle of white pills. There was writing on the side. " 'Humidifier tablets,' " Marcy read. " 'Drop one in tank of humidifier per week to have clean, fresh-smelling water.' "

My mother looked shocked. Then she really began to laugh. She couldn't stop laughing!

Gus had torn his open, too, and held up something with buttons and a bulb. He had some long black thing around his neck.

"What is it?" he said. "What is this thing?"

Now my mom was bent over and red in the face. "It's a blood-pressure kit," she blurted out. "Grandma left it here on her last visit!"

I began to get nervous. I felt like this had something to do with me.

"Tony wrapped the wrong boxes," she shrieked. "It was my fault. I was in a hurry and I didn't show him which ones."

Leave it to me to ruin Christmas.

My mom ran and got the right presents. She didn't even wrap them. She put her arm around me.

Marcy and Gus were roaring now too.

"Tony, you made the day. If we had planned a joke like that, it wouldn't have worked," said my mom.

I guess I was just a funny guy.

"Merry Merry Huckleberry!" my mom

117

said, from the pile of wrapping paper and bows we were sitting in.

"The same to you," I said.

And I meant it.